Dear Parents and Educators,

W9-BMB-947

Welcome to Penguin Young Readers! As parents and educators, you know that each child develops at his or her own pace—in terms of speech, critical thinking, and, of course, reading. Penguin Young Readers recognizes this fact. As a result, each Penguin Young Readers book is assigned a traditional easy-to-read level (1–4) as well as a Guided Reading Level (A–P). Both of these systems will help you choose the right book for your child. Please refer to the back of each book for specific leveling information. Penguin Young Readers features esteemed authors and illustrators, stories about favorite characters, fascinating nonfiction, and more!

Young Cam Jansen and the Baseball Mystery

LEVEL **3**

GUIDED
READING
LEVEL **J**

This book is perfect for a **Transitional Reader** who:
- can read multisyllable and compound words;
- can read words with prefixes and suffixes;
- is able to identify story elements (beginning, middle, end, plot, setting, characters, problem, solution); and
- can understand different points of view.

Here are some **activities** you can do during and after reading this book:
- Compound Words: A compound word is made when two words are joined together to form a new word. Baseball, for example, is a compound word. Reread the story and try to find other compound words.
- Adding -ing to Words: There are many rules when adding -ing to words: If a word ends with a vowel and then a consonant, repeat the consonant before adding -ing: hum/humming. If a word ends with an e, delete it before adding -ing: skate/skating. If a word ends with two vowels and then a consonant, just add -ing: clean/cleaning. If a word ends with a y, just add -ing: say/saying. Find the -ing words in the story. On a separate sheet of paper, write the -ing word and the root word next to it. Then identify the rule above that applies to each word.

Remember, sharing the love of reading with a child is the best gift you can give!

—Bonnie Bader, EdM
   Penguin Young Readers program

*Penguin Young Readers are leveled by independent reviewers applying the standards developed by Irene Fountas and Gay Su Pinnell in *Matching Books to Readers: Using Leveled Books in Guided Reading*, Heinemann, 1999.

For Aliza, Uri, Dovid, Shlomo, and Ilana—DA

To Emma Willsky—SN

Penguin Young Readers
Published by the Penguin Group
Penguin Group (USA) Inc., 375 Hudson Street, New York, New York 10014, USA
Penguin Group (Canada), 90 Eglinton Avenue East, Suite 700, Toronto, Ontario M4P 2Y3, Canada
(a division of Pearson Penguin Canada Inc.)
Penguin Books Ltd., 80 Strand, London WC2R 0RL, England
Penguin Group Ireland, 25 St. Stephen's Green, Dublin 2, Ireland (a division of Penguin Books Ltd.)
Penguin Group (Australia), 250 Camberwell Road, Camberwell, Victoria 3124, Australia
(a division of Pearson Australia Group Pty. Ltd.)
Penguin Books India Pvt. Ltd., 11 Community Centre, Panchsheel Park, New Delhi—110 017, India
Penguin Group (NZ), 67 Apollo Drive, Rosedale, Auckland 0632, New Zealand
(a division of Pearson New Zealand Ltd.)
Penguin Books (South Africa) (Pty.) Ltd., 24 Sturdee Avenue, Rosebank,
Johannesburg 2196, South Africa

Penguin Books Ltd., Registered Offices: 80 Strand, London WC2R 0RL, England

Text copyright © 1999 by David A. Adler. Illustrations copyright © 1999 by Susanna Natti. All rights
reserved. First published in 1999 by Viking and in 2001 by Puffin Books, imprints of Penguin Group
(USA) Inc. Published in 2012 by Penguin Young Readers, an imprint of Penguin Group (USA) Inc.,
345 Hudson Street, New York, New York 10014. Manufactured in China.

The Library of Congress has cataloged the Viking edition
under the following Control Number: 98035726

ISBN 978-0-14-131106-7   10 9 8 7 6 5 4 3 2

Young Cam Jansen
and the Baseball Mystery

by David A. Adler
illustrated by Susanna Natti

Penguin Young Readers
An Imprint of Penguin Group (USA) Inc.

Contents

Chapter 1
Play Ball!

"Watch out!"

Cam Jansen called

to her friend Eric Shelton.

"Why?" Eric asked.

They were walking in a park.

Splash!

Eric stepped into a puddle.

"That's why," Cam told him.

The park was crowded.

People were sitting on benches.

Some were reading.

Some were talking.

Some were resting.

Children were riding bicycles

and flying kites.

"Watch out!" Cam said again.

Eric looked down.

He wasn't about to step into

a puddle.

"Why?" Eric asked.

Just then a red ball flew by.

It almost hit him.

"That's why," Cam told Eric.

"Watch out!" Cam said a third time.

A dog was playing catch

with an old man.

The dog almost ran into Eric.

It ran to the red ball.

Then it picked up the ball in its teeth

and ran back with it.

Eric was careful.

He watched where he walked.

He watched the kites and the

children riding bicycles.

Cam and Eric walked to the

edge of the baseball field.

"There's Robert," Cam said.

She pointed.

"And there's Rachel."

Robert and Rachel were on the

baseball field.

Some of Cam and Eric's other

friends were there, too.

Cam and Eric hurried over.

"I'm glad you're here," Robert
told them.

"I brought a bat."

"And I brought a ball," Rachel said.

"But we still don't have enough
players."

Robert said, "A lot of people told
me they would come.

I had a list of them all,
but I left it at school."

"I saw the list," Cam said.

She closed her eyes and said, "Click!"

Cam always closes her eyes
and says, "Click!"

when she wants to remember
something.

Cam has an amazing memory.
"My memory is like a camera,"
she said.
"I have a picture in my head
of everything I've seen.
Click! is the sound my camera makes."
Cam's eyes were still closed.

"I'm looking at the list," she said.
Then she opened her eyes.
"Jane, Annie, and Evan were on
the list.

They're not here yet."

Cam's real name is Jennifer.

But because of her great memory

people started calling her

"the Camera."

Then "the Camera"

became just "Cam."

Cam, Eric, and their friends waited.

Then Jane, Annie, and Evan

all came at the same time.

Robert and Rachel divided everyone

into two teams.

Then Robert called out,

"Play ball!"

Chapter 2
Home Run!

Cam and Eric were on Robert's team.

They were on the field

at the start of the game.

The first batter hit the ball

high into the air.

Robert ran back.

He reached up and caught it.

"One out!" he called.

The next batter

hit the ball onto the ground.

Cam reached down for the ball.

She threw it to Eric at first base.

"Two outs!" Robert called.

Then Amy came to bat.

"Move back," Robert told his team.

Amy swung hard at the first pitch
and missed.

"Strike one!" Robert called.

Amy swung hard at the second
pitch, too, and missed.

"Strike two!" Robert called.

Amy looked out at the pitcher
and waited.

She swung hard at the third pitch.

She hit the ball high over
Robert's head.

Amy ran to first base.

Robert ran back for the ball.

Amy ran to second base.

Robert kept running back.

Amy ran to third base.

Robert ran off the baseball field.

He ran past some children
who were flying kites.

Robert ran to where
people were sitting on benches.

He stopped and looked for the ball.

Amy ran home.

"Home run!" Amy shouted.

"I hit a home run!"

Her team cheered.

Rachel took the bat.

She stood at home plate.

Everyone waited for Robert

to throw the ball to the pitcher.

"Hurry! Hurry!" Rachel called.

"I want to hit a home run, too."

Robert ran back onto the field.

"I can't find it," he called.

"I can't find the ball!"

Chapter 3
There It Is

Cam closed her eyes and said,

"Click!"

"The ball went over Robert's head,"

she said.

"It bounced near a tree."

Cam opened her eyes.

She pointed to a tree at the edge

of the baseball field.

"That's the one," she said.

Cam, Eric, and the others ran to

the tree.

They looked for the ball.

"I see it. I see it," Rachel said.

She ran past the tree and picked

something up.

"No, it's not the ball," she said.

"It's just a rolled-up piece of paper."

Dara pointed to something near

a bench.

"There's a ball," she said.

"But it's not ours. It's red."

Eric looked at a puddle.

"This looks deep," he said.

"Maybe the ball is in here."

Eric found a branch on the ground.

He used it to poke in the puddle.

"Hey!" he called out.

"I found something."

Eric used the branch to push it out
of the puddle.

"It's not the ball," Eric said.

"It's just an empty soda can."

"There it is," Robert said.

"I found it."

He pointed to a girl and boy
who were playing catch.

Robert said, "They're playing with
our ball."

Chapter 4
That's Our Ball

The girl threw the ball high

over the boy's head.

The boy jumped, but he didn't catch it.

He turned, ran, and stopped the ball

with his foot.

Just then Cam remembered something.

The boy picked the ball up.

Cam closed her eyes and said, "Click!"

Robert walked over to the girl and boy.

Eric, Rachel, and the others

followed him.

"That's our ball," Robert said.

"Amy hit it over my head

and you found it.

Now we want it back."

Cam opened her eyes.

She looked at the benches.

She looked at the people sitting

on them.

Cam closed her eyes again

and said, "Click!"

"This ball is ours," the girl said.

"We brought it from home."

Robert held out his hand and said,

"Let me see it."

The girl gave the ball to Robert.

He showed it to Rachel.

"Is this yours?" he asked.

Rachel looked at the ball and said,

"No. It's not. I wrote my name on

the ball."

She gave the ball back to the girl.

"I'm sorry," Robert said.

"I was wrong.

It's not our ball."

Rachel told Robert and the others,

"Let's keep looking."

"No," Cam said and opened her eyes.

"We don't have to look for the ball.

We have to look for a dog."

Chapter 5
Ruff! Ruff!

"That's silly," Rachel said.

"We didn't lose a dog.

We lost a ball."

Cam led them to the red ball.

"I found that before," Dara said.

"It's not ours."

Eric told Cam, "Our ball is white."

Cam picked up the red ball.

She showed it to her friends.

"Do you see the teeth marks

in this ball?" she asked.

"An old man was playing catch with his dog."

"That's right," Eric said.

"First the ball almost hit me. Then the dog almost ran into me."

"This is all very nice," Rachel said.

"But I want to find my ball."

Cam said, "I think the old man threw this ball.

The dog ran for it.

But it took back Rachel's ball.

That's why this red ball was left
near the bench.

We should look for the dog.

It's small, brown, and has white spots.

If we find that dog,
we'll find Rachel's ball."

"No," Robert said.

"Let's just keep looking for
Rachel's ball."

Robert and some of the children
kept looking for the ball.
Cam, Eric, Rachel, and Evan
looked for the dog.
They found it in the open field.
It was running to the old man.
There was a ball in its mouth.
Cam, Eric, Rachel, and Evan
ran to the old man, too.

The old man took the ball

out of the dog's mouth.

It was a white ball.

He was about to throw it.

"Stop!" Cam called to him.

"Don't throw the ball."

He stopped.

He didn't throw the ball.

"That's mine," Rachel told the man.

Cam gave him the red ball.

"This is yours," she said.

The old man looked at

the red and white balls.

"The white one has a name on it.

Are you Rachel?" the man asked.

"Yes," Rachel told him.

"Then this is yours," the man said.

He gave Rachel the white ball.

"I'm sorry we had it.

I wasn't watching what ball
Pal brought back."

Ruff! Ruff! Pal barked.

Rachel ran to Robert
and showed him the ball.

"You were right," Robert told Cam.

"Let's play ball," Rachel said.

She walked to home plate.

"Pitch it here," Rachel said.

"I want to hit a home run."

A Cam Jansen Memory Game

Take another look at the picture on page 4.
Study it.
Blink your eyes and say, **"Click!"**
Then turn back to this page
and answer these questions:

1. Who is in front, Cam or Eric?

2. What color are Eric's sneakers?

3. How many kites are in the picture?

4. Who is stepping in a puddle?